Copyright 2024 by Meret Bitticks

All rights reserved. No part of this book may be reproduced or used in any manner without written permission from the author or publisher, except as permitted by U.S. copyright law.

Cover Design and Interior Design by Ophelia Barrett

ISBN 978-1-63991-117-2

ISBN

Published by F-flat Books.

Philadelphia, PA www.fflat-books.com

www.meretbitticks.com

Introduction

My 6th grade band director wrangled 15 beginning percussionists and still found time to play a flute duet (that he arranged!) with me on my first ever band concert. He patiently taught me to put my flute together and how to produce a tone on the instrument. I am in awe of the depth and breadth of knowledge band directors have at their fingertips. And yet, many multi-instrumentalists have expressed to me both the difficulty of playing the flute as well as troubleshooting beginners. This observation is reinforced for me every time I walk in to teach a new Flute Methods class for Music Education majors at DePaul University. How do we form an embouchure without a mouthpiece? What's the best first fingering to teach for B-flat? And exactly how do we prevent ourselves from knocking the person next to us in the ear when we bring the flute up?

This book is the culmination of 20 years of working with flute beginners from ages 3 to 80, as well as their teachers, in my role as a Suzuki Flute Teacher Trainer and is dedicated to the generation of DePaul students who have since become colleagues. I am deeply indebted to my own teachers and mentors, in particular, Katherine Borst Jones, Mary Stolper, David Royce-Gerry, and Kelly Williamson.

How To Use This Book

There are many well-known method books for flute to help people improve their flute playing. This is not one of them. While the tips in this book may ultimately help your own playing, this book seeks to help improve people's flute teaching in a user-friendly encyclopedia-style reference format. Information will be presented in short paragraphs and categorized under large topic headings and smaller subheadings. When appropriate, links for video demonstrations will also be included. For example, if a student walks in one day with newly installed braces and can no longer get a note out of the instrument, go to "Tone Production" and then "Braces" to read my tried-and-true trick for helping students with orthodontic impediments. Sometimes we assume an issue is wholly the fault of the student, when in fact the instrument is not in good repair. The troubleshooting tips in this book presuppose that there is not a mechanical reason for the problem (that's a long way of saying "check the screws, springs, and eyeball the pads!")

QR codes are linked to corresponding videos.

Topics

Embouchure Formation — 6

  Headjoint Anatomy
  Rice "Spitting"
  Start With Headjoint Only
  The Five Variables of Headjoint Placement

Posture / Position — 12

  Flute Alignment
  Balance Points
  Body Posture
  Hand Position
  Sitting and Standing
  Breathing
  Curved Headjoint and Waveline™ Flutes

Tone Production — 20

  Air Speed / Amount / Direction
  Weak Tone
  Airy Tone
  Middle Register
  Wrong Register (Too High or Too Low)
  Third Register
  Buzzing Lips
  Support
  Dynamics
  Vibrato

Articulation — 30

- Between vs. Behind The Teeth
- Tongue Placement
- Fuzzy Attacks
- Note Endings
- Coordination of Tongue and Fingers
- Double Tonguing

Intonation — 38

- Tuning the Instrument
- Intonation Tendencies
- Headjoint Cork
- Some Problematic Notes (C#, F#, G#)
- Harmonics
- Ways to Adjust While Playing

Technique — 44

- Finger Order
- B-Flats
- Contrary Motion (C-D-E)
- Left Pointer "Herbert"
- Hitchhiker Notes
- Common Fingering Issues

Piccolo — 50

- Types of Piccolos
- Tone Production
- Intonation
- Buzzing Lips

First, a word on tone. Much emphasis is placed on getting a "sound" out of the instrument as quickly as possible. I am on the parent-side of this equation right now as the mother of a five-year-old aspiring flutist and I can attest to the frustration when something doesn't work out and how exciting a sound, any sound, can be when it squawks out of the headjoint. Only later do we get around to asking why the student's tone is inconsistent or they have trouble changing registers. In these early days, it can be hard to remember that ultimately we are helping our students develop a strong flute tone when they pick up the instrument. Let's make sure that we are not accepting future headaches in exchange for instant gratification.

When working with a total beginner, understanding some basic principles will ensure that when the flute comes up to their face they will meet with success. Every beginner I work with, regardless of their age or musical experience starts the same way: spitting rice first, then playing the headjoint only, with special attention to placement on the lip.

Headjoint Anatomy

The headjoint is the part of the flute that produces sound. Here are some important terms for identifying the parts of the headjoint:

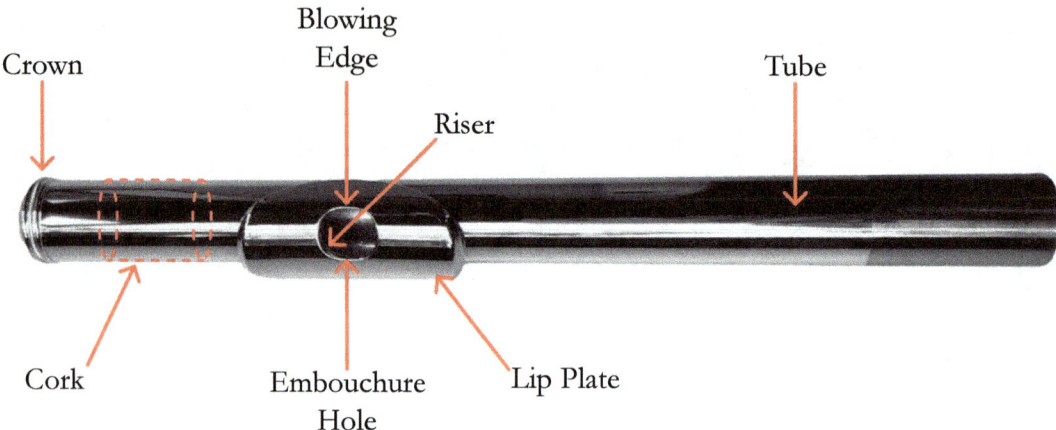

Rice "Spitting"

Tone production on the flute is nebulous and requires movements and control of muscles that most students have never had to do prior to picking up the instrument. Rice spitting is a technique used in the Suzuki flute world to help young children form a natural embouchure and articulate the starts of notes, but works beautifully with players of all ages. This technique mimics the French style of tonguing, or saying the word "tu" in French. Having something physical, like rice, allows students to feel the release of the air by the tongue while keeping their mouths in a natural, neutral position (ideal for tone production). This can be a fun activity for the early days of the school year when it's nice outside (it makes a mess!) but I've known people to have success with students simply imagining the action ("imagine you're spitting watermelon seeds at a picnic"). Most 4th-6th grade beginners will not require the technique to be broken down into its five component parts, but here they are for the sake of clarity:

1. Breathe in
2. Hold the air
3. Place tongue just peeking out between lips
4. Place rice on tongue
5. Pull tongue back, releasing air and sending rice out

Start With Headjoint Only

Most flute teachers (myself included) have beginners start with the headjoint only, as it reduces the number of factors teacher and student have to troubleshoot. There are many activities that can be done with only a headjoint that work in a group or one-on-one setting, such as:

Rhythms: Clap or play rhythms for students to imitate in a call-and-response format. Particularly useful for introducing any tricky rhythms for upcoming pieces.

Long note contests: which student can hold the note the longest on a headjoint?

High/low tones: There are a variety of sounds that can be produced on the headjoint, including placing a hand over the open end of the headjoint tube to get a lower sound. This can be combined with the call-and-response activity to help them begin to differentiate pitch. (Incidentally the note the headjoint produces is an "A." There are now some short pieces that have been written for headjoint and piano!)

Random Repetitions: I like to randomize the number of "toots" I have students play by rolling dice, spinning a number wheel, or choosing a playing card. Having students do shorter bursts of toots, putting the headjoint down, and then picking it up again to do another set of toots reinforces the headjoint placement and muscle memory. We hope our students never zone out, but if they do, we want them to be able to snap-to and begin playing without a lot of adjusting or fuss.

The Five Variables of Headjoint Placement

As it turns out, where the headjoint is placed on a lip has a lot to do with the quality of tone (if any at all) that is produced. Flute headjoints always have their open end to the right side of the flute player and the crown to the left. Most makers have a thicker and thinner side to the lip plate and in those cases the thicker side goes against the flutist's chin. Generally, the embouchure hole should be placed centered on and perpendicular to (right angle) the nose, with the near edge of the embouchure hole about at the edge of the lower lip (this may need to be adjusted slightly higher for very full lips or slightly lower for very thin lips, but is a good place to start). The far edge, or "blowing edge" of the embouchure hole should be just visible if you're looking straight on at the student.

Below are the five variables of headjoint placement. I rarely actually list them for a beginner, however, I do find that knowing them helps me in the troubleshooting process. Any changes in where the headjoint is placed on the lip will result in a change of where the air hits the blowing edge of the embouchure hole, potentially changing intonation, register, and clarity of the tone.

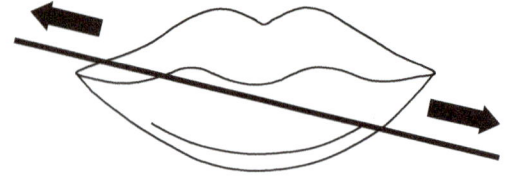

1. Angle to the floor: The headjoint should be parallel to the lip opening and perpendicular to the nose.

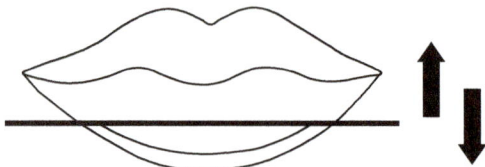

2. High/low on lip: The embouchure hole should be at the bottom edge of lip.

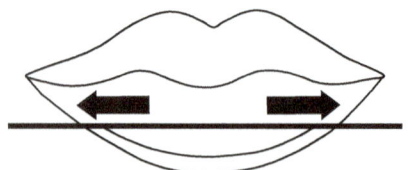

3. Right/left centering on lip: center the embouchure hole on nose.

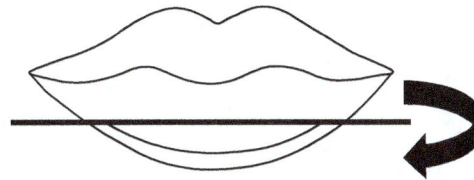

4. Rolling in or out: the embouchure hole is "rolled in" if too much of it is facing the student, rolled out if more than the blowing edge is visible.

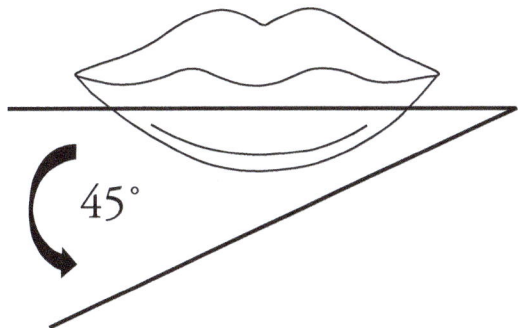

5. Angle of the flute (or headjoint) from shoulder: the flute should make a 45 degree angle to the shoulder.

From time to time a student will have a pronounced dip or "teardrop" in the middle of their upper lip. Many times the rice spitting exercise is all it takes for the student to learn to flatten their lip out enough to not affect their embouchure. Having the student say the word "pure" will also help them raise the middle of their upper lip. There are many fine flutists who prevent the teardrop from bisecting their airstream by playing off to one side or the other. It may take some experimentation but a teardrop lip does not need to be a deal-breaker for flutists.

Special note for marching band: traditional marching bands often like their flutists to have the flute completely parallel to their shoulder. While this looks great, it does change the way the air moves across the blowing edge of the embouchure hole as well as create tension and bad habits off the football field. Whenever possible, I advise my students to play piccolo for marching band - they can be heard better outside and it eliminates the angle issue.

Posture/Position

We don't know if the student in front of us will go on to become a professional musician or choose another path, but our responsibility is to set every kid up to be successful for whatever path they choose. This of course means guarding the health of the tendons and muscles that play the instrument, but apart from their overall well-being, posture tremendously affects the quality of the tone as well as intonation on the flute. A healthy position begins with aligning the flute in such a way that allows the flutist to hold an unnatural instrument as naturally as possible. Developing a relaxed and natural hand position, learning how to sit and when (and how) to stand, and how to breathe efficiently and effectively are foundational to their future flute playing.

Flutists with shorter arm lengths may have trouble holding a traditionally designed flute comfortably. Curved headjoint or Waveline™ flutes shorten the distance a player's arms have to stretch from their bodies without changing pitch or tone, discussed more in-depth in the last section.

Flute Alignment

I align the headjoint of the flute so that the majority of the keys on the body are facing straight up at the ceiling and the flute is parallel to the ceiling and floor. This keeps the flute at a 90 degree angle from the nose. (The flute can go down, but then the head must also tilt down.) The weight of the mechanism comes from one side, where the rods connect the keys. Flutists must always be mindful to ensure that the weight of the keys is not causing the flute to roll inward towards them.

Headjoint: How the headjoint is placed into the body of the flute is critical to a student making a strong, clear tone on the flute while holding the instrument in a way that will be healthy for their hands.

Some makers etch alignment markers on the headjoint and barrel of the body - don't trust these. The "neutral" placement of the headjoint aligns the center of the embouchure hole with the center of the "A" key on the body of the flute. Some flutists have their embouchure holes "rolled in" from there, or with the hole slightly more towards them. Others "roll out." When a flutist hasn't yet developed a strong preference (aka is a beginner) I think it's best to line the embouchure up as close to the center of the "A" key as possible. This will allow them to make sure the keys on the body of the flute are looking up at the ceiling and not rolling in towards the flutist or out towards the audience, either of which would cause the hands to take a position that could ultimately result in injury such as tendonitis or carpal tunnel syndrome. When I find a headjoint position I like I mark the headjoint and body with nail polish so that I can easily find the right alignment (for both myself and my students).

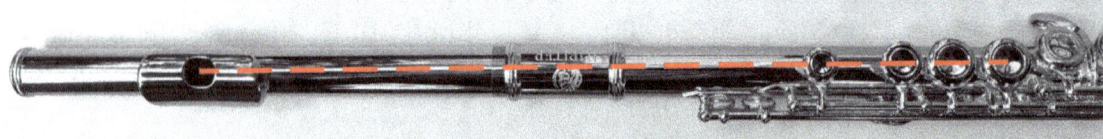

Footjoint: The rod on the footjoint should be aligned with the center of the right hand keys. Many students want the rods on the body and footjoint to line up with one another, which puts the pinky keys far too low to use comfortably. More commonly, I see students who want the pinky keys to be on the same plane as the right hand body keys. This works okay until they have to play low notes and move their pinkies from the default D-sharp key.

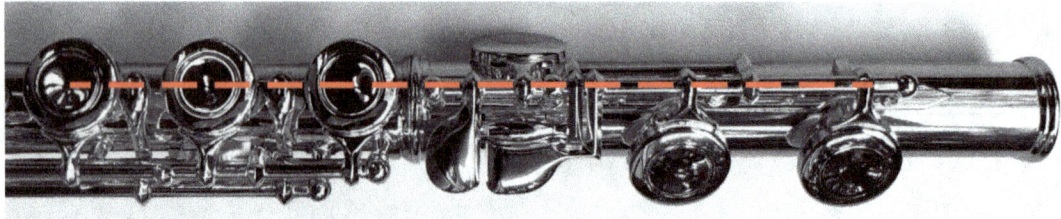

Balance Points

For beginning flutists holding the flute can be an exercise in faith. There are three balance points when holding the instrument: the chin; the metacarpophalangeal joint (first knuckle) of the left index finger; and the right thumb. The chin anchors the flute to the body, the left knuckle counterbalances that by holding it in place from the other side. The right thumb keeps the flute up. Some people assume that the right pinky counterbalances the thumb by pushing down from the top of the flute, but that can lead to what I call "the iron pinky of death" or the kid jamming it down as hard as possible, potentially causing injury. The weight of the pinky should be all that is needed to depress the D-sharp key. It is possible to loosen the spring on that key if it is too stiff.

Body Posture

Balanced posture in life equals balanced posture on flute. Flutists with inconsistent posture have inconsistent tone and intonation. Any change in the flutist's head, arms, hands, or spine will change one or more of the five variables of headjoint placement, thus changing the way the air moves across the blowing edge of the embouchure hole. Insisting on proper body alignment not only allows students to play better and more consistently, it also protects their growing bodies and ensures long-term health.

Spine: Tension-free posture, whether sitting or standing, begins with making sure our spine is in a neutral, "stacked" position. We know the spine is not a straight line, but a median line can be drawn through the natural curves close to the center of our bodies. This allows the head to balance over the center of gravity (not "tech-neck") as though being held up by an invisible string from the crown of the head. The string image allows the student to adjust themselves without needing hands-on help from me. Having them wiggle around a bit also helps things settle and gives you a chance to eyeball whether the student is hyper extending or slouching.

Shoulders: Once the spine is stacked and tall, the next area for potential disaster becomes the shoulders. Many people hear "shoulders back!" and squeeze their shoulder blades together from the middle of their upper back, thrusting their chest out and creating tension in their armpits that can radiate down the arm. I tell my students to have "yoga shoulders" or to roll their shoulders up and back, allowing the shoulder blades to hang. This method opens up the upper chest and allows the arms to lift without lifting the shoulders. One bonus: young flutists with developing chests can be sensitive and slouch in an effort to disguise their changing body. Yoga shoulders allow the lungs freedom to expand without the flutist feeling like they're pushing themselves out and on display.

Some students raise their shoulders up a lot when they pick up the flute. The easiest way to counteract this is often to have them raise their shoulders to "touch" their ears, and then let them drop down.

Pelvis: Just as we seek a neutral spine, we also look for a pelvis that is tilted neither too far forward or too far back. Most kids seem to tilt their pelvis forward by default. This is most noticeable when they're standing, although it can be the start of slouching when seated.

Whole books have been written on posture alone and Alexander Technique experts are an invaluable resource. Lea Pearson's book, *Body Mapping for Flutists* is a comprehensive dive into these ideas.

Hand Position

My students and I joke that they should have "banana fingers." No one wants to eat a banana that's stick straight, nor one that is gnarled and curled up. Asking our fingers to stay in the center of the key will help troubleshoot our balance points as well as allow for free and easy movement from the first knuckles, especially in the right hand. Be alert for students with hypermobility in their finger joints - it will be extra important for them to focus on keeping a gentle curve in the fingers (especially pinky) and to keep an eye on their right thumb.

Left: The left hand position on the flute starts with the left index first knuckle against and slightly under the body of the flute, near the B key. The exact placement of the knuckle is determined by the size of the hand, but we want to make sure that the thumb is free to move on and off the thumb mechanism and can stay straight. The left palm is going to be open and facing the body of the flute so that the fingers can naturally fall in the center of the keys.

Right: My mentor, David Gerry, used to say you can find your right hand position at the end of your right arm. As simplistic as this sounds, the way someone's wrist and hand lines up when resting at their side is exactly the way it should be when holding a flute. Same for the right thumb: for most people, the right thumb wants to be under their index finger, or possibly slightly between the index and middle fingers. When in doubt, have a student shake out their hand down at their side and see where the thumb ends up. The movement of the fingers comes from the big first (metacarpophalangeal) knuckles and the palm opens towards the flute. This becomes impossible if the thumb is too far forward, which causes the fingers to either overlap the keys or have to have a tall bend to stay centered on the key. Many students want to rotate their hand up towards the headjoint, but rotating it ever so slightly towards the footjoint lengthens the pinky and gives it more freedom of movement.

A special note about right thumb and pinky: In general, hypermobility in finger joints is totally manageable for flutists. Two areas of concern are the thumb and pinky of the right hand. Many people have "hitchhiker's thumbs" or have hypermobility in the top joint of their thumb. I think having the thumb sit where it wants to naturally is a really good place to start, but if students are holding the flute in such a way that it promotes an extreme bend I will try to find a placement that allows it to stay straighter.

As mentioned earlier, some students jam their pinkies down to the point of hyperextending the top joint in what I call "iron pinky of death." My pinky was so strong that I actually bent the tenon of my footjoint and caused the footjoint to fall off in a concert! Fortunately, with a little attention (and potential lightening of that D-sharp key spring), keeping a curve in that pinky is totally doable. The D-sharp key should be depressed for virtually every note except for D, so that pinky will get a lot of practice staying curved.

Sitting and Standing

Sitting is the standard when playing flute in an ensemble setting whereas standing is preferred for solo performances. Students like to prop their right elbow up on the back of their chair, causing their pelvis to tilt forward and their spine to curve, resulting in slouching flutists. I advise students to sit near the front of the chair with both feet on the ground, which solves this problem. One of the hardest parts of setting up a flute section for an ensemble is to figure out how to fit the number of flutists in with enough real estate for the instrument to stick out two feet from the player. I like to angle the chairs with a shared stand in the middle so that the flutes are never in the same plane.

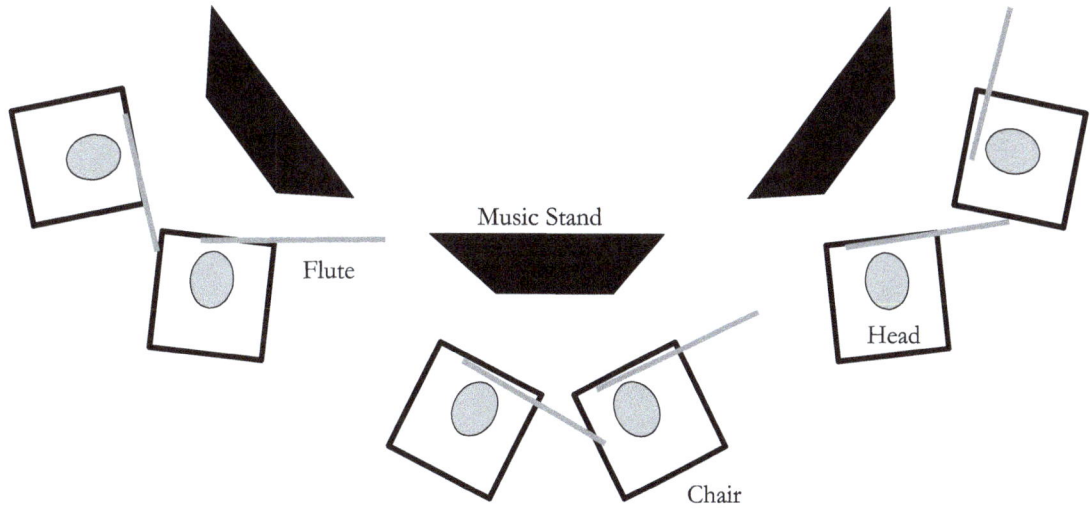

When standing I like to have the student's left foot pointed towards whatever they're looking at (a music stand or the audience) with the right foot about hip's width apart at an angle. Some teachers like the feet to point in the same direction. Regardless, the important thing is for the pelvis and spine to be aligned and to allow for a 45 degree angle between the right shoulder and flute. When set up this way the flute will be parallel with the music stand. This position also enables the rib cage to expand freely when breathing.

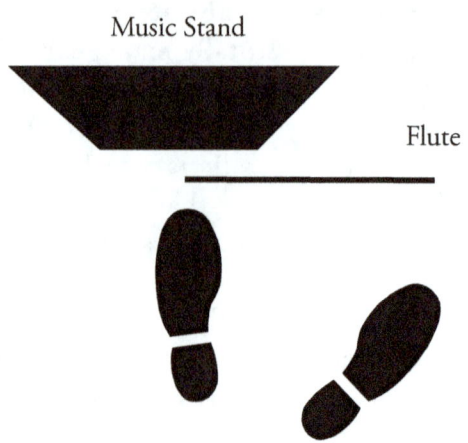

Breathing

For something that everyone does all day every day, breathing can be remarkably hard to teach. It is also completely dependent on a person's posture: our lungs work much harder to take in air when we slouch. Because so much of our air goes across and not into the instrument, and because of the lack of back-pressure coming from the instrument, flutists need to take in as much air as they possibly can. Much like posture, there are many experts who have devoted their lives to understanding how to breathe more efficiently. There seem to be as many breathing exercises as stars in the sky. That said, here are a few small tips that have helped my young students.

Balloons: I love using balloons as visuals for my students (they're also great for repetitions, but that's for another time!) The lungs are, in essence, a balloon. When our lungs expand, they expand both in front and in back as well as up and down. Have students pair up and take turns "breathing into" one another's hands, which are hovering over (not touching) the breather's shoulder blades.

Open throat: Many of us hold our breath by closing our throat in what linguists call a "glottal stop." This action is not necessary to keep the air in our bodies; all that is necessary is to not allow our lungs to deflate. "If you never close your throat you never have to open your throat" is flippant but also very true. This can be a better concept for more advanced players, but would be worth exploring if you hear a lot of noisy breathing coming from your flute section. Bonus - it tends to help tone as well.

Footjoint breaths: Have your flutists remove their footjoint and put the end (pinky keys away from them) in their mouths with their fingers closing any open keys. Breathing in through this tube is very effective for showing students how to open their throats and take a lot of air in quickly.

Curved Headjoint and Waveline™ Flutes

In an effort to accommodate flutists of varying sizes, instrument makers have made curved headjoints, in which a regular student flute headjoint is replaced by one that curves up and over the body of the flute. Curved headjoints can be used interchangeably with traditional straight headjoints on any flute body, as long as the tube diameter is the same. Most students have no trouble learning to balance the flute with a curved headjoint, but they can be a little wobbly in the beginning. More recently, Jupiter® has invented their proprietary Waveline™ flute, which replaces the stacked curve with a "wave" that hangs below the flute. The Waveline™ solves the balance issue that can come with using a curved headjoint, but with the sacrifice of making the body of the flute shorter. This means Waveline™ flutes can only be used with Waveline™ headjoints (straight or waved). Modified headjoint flutes are absolutely necessary for very young players, and many of my students use theirs until they're in late elementary school. Some petite flutists may appreciate using them even longer.

Flutists who switch to a straight headjoint too soon must straighten their right arm and then bend at the wrist to access the right-hand mechanism. Some flutists who transfer to me and exhibit this tendency express great relief at making the switch to a modified headjoint. Others are very resistant. This may be best left to a private flute teacher, when possible, but your support will help ensure the success of any transition.

The important thing to know is that even if these flutes look a little funny, they sound absolutely the same as a regular student flute. Possibly better, because they allow the flutist to have better posture. When a student gets antsy about switching to a straight headjoint, I ask them to put the flute up as if they were going to play, but to move their right hand to hold the end of the footjoint. If they can do that while keeping a bend in their right arm I know the arm is long enough to hold a flute with a straight headjoint.

Tone Production

Our tone is our voice. Tone forms the basis for our musical expression and can make playing so much more fun and rewarding. It is the first thing that people notice when we play and frankly a resonant tone hides all manner of sins. Once the foundation for the embouchure and posture is formed, refinements to air speed, amount, and direction can either solve or create problems with weak and/or airy tone. Experienced players calibrate their air depending on the sound they hope to achieve. Learning to manage the speed and direction of air gives students control over their middle register, dynamics, and vibrato. We will also discuss what to do when a student's playing is affected by braces.

Air Speed / Amount / Direction

The work of the flutist is to learn to control their air speed, amount, and direction. The possibility for more nuance and more control presents itself at the start of every practice session. These three variables can be adjusted individually but ultimately work together to allow the flutist to change register, tone color, dynamics, and intonation.

Air speed: How fast is the air cutting across the blowing edge of the embouchure hole? Every flutist needs to learn the minimum speed of air necessary to cause the instrument to resonate and create tone. If the air is too slow no sound will come out. Too fast, and the flutist runs the risk of overblowing, or having a harmonic unintentionally pop out. Much like the tuning pegs and fine tuners on string instruments, we have a more macro and a micro option to adjust air speed. Support through the engagement of core muscles can enact large scale change. For finer adjustments, a larger embouchure aperture will slow down the speed of air, much as a river's current gets slower as it gets wider. A smaller embouchure will have the opposite effect.

Air amount: How much air is being used? This can affect the speed of the air (more air usually equals faster air) but it is possible to divorce the two by adjusting the size of the embouchure aperture. It is a much lamented truth of the instrument that much of the air we blow across the embouchure hole never makes it into the flute. Many students default to not using enough air (this manifests as the "it's my sound, you can't hear it" school of flute playing as my mentor David Gerry used to say). Others use a lot of air inefficiently, becoming lightheaded and unable to control their register.

Air direction: Where does the air go? In general, the lower a player can aim their air, the more air will get into the flute, resulting in a bigger, clearer tone. Taken to the extreme, this can counterproductively produce a "covered" and less powerful sound. There are many compelling reasons to have embouchure flexibility and the ability to raise the airstream such as playing softly and changing register (or both!) Some teachers have students change air direction by bringing the jaw down and back or out and forward. Others concentrate on making all the changes with the lips. I've found that for myself, I have to move my jaw, but for both myself and my students I encourage the smallest possible movement that still achieves the desired result. I do this mostly for the health of the Temporomandibular joint (TMJ), but also for the sake of efficiency. For this reason I tend to talk more about where I think the air should go and less about how I think they should make it get there. Students can have a hard time with the abstraction of this, so it can be helpful to give them something physical at which to aim their air such as a location in the room or their hand.

Putting it together: Imagine you're playing catch with someone. If you don't throw the ball hard enough it will fall to the ground, never making it to them. If you throw it down to the ground it doesn't matter how hard you throw, it will also never make it to your partner. If your partner moves closer, you'll probably want to throw the ball more gently so you don't knock them over. If they move further away, you'll probably want to angle the ball up and throw harder to ensure that it makes it to them. If you found yourself suddenly tossing about a basketball instead of a softball, the same throw would yield a slower ball.

A physical manifestation of this, using the instrument, comes through the harmonic series. As the airstream rises (and usually gets faster), the flutist produces an octave, then a fifth, then a fourth above that (the next octave), then a major third, and on the lowest fingerings, a minor third. Keeping the same fingering allows a student to focus on their air and can then be applied to the standard fingering.

Weak Tone

Usually a weak tone is the result of the student not using enough air. Remember that much of the air a flutist blows across the embouchure hole never actually makes it into the instrument. Assuming that the headjoint seems to be optimally aligned on the lip (and that the headjoint is not rolled too far in or out on the flute), the solution for a weak tone is usually for the student to increase the amount of their air, thus increasing the speed of their air. (See "Air Speed / Amount / Direction" for an in-depth discussion about how these two are related and can be adjusted) Another trick that can work well is to have the student imagine they're aiming their air at their left elbow (no fair bringing the elbow up!) which will help direct more air down into the instrument.

Airy Tone

Sometimes a flutist has a strong sound, but it is not a clear sound. There is "fuzz" or "air" around the edges. There are two primary causes for this: 1. The aperture of the flutist's embouchure is too open, allowing a lot of air to escape and/or 2. Ironically, the flutist is not using enough air.

A wide oval embouchure, visible when you face the flutist, is a clear indication that the aperture is too open. Another way to check is to look at the vapor stream left on the metal (easiest to see if you clean a spot on the headjoint and actually have them blow somewhere on the tube, not on the lip plate). If the vapor trail is very wide, then their aperture is probably too open. Having the student spit rice is a sure-fire way to narrow the aperture without creating tension. Other exercises could include having the student blow "hot" (open mouth) vs "cool" (narrow opening) on their own hand to feel the difference. The soda straw can be a useful visual as can talking about different sized foods/candy to help them close their lips more ("pretend you're holding a "nerd" candy between your lips").

Some students hear the air in the sound and assume they're using too much air when in fact they need more. Without achieving a certain amount of speed cutting across the blowing edge of the embouchure hole and getting a certain amount of air down into the instrument the sound will always be airy. This can still be a function of having an open embouchure (the wider the opening the slower the air) but usually it benefits from having a student use more air when they play.

Middle Register

In a perfect world, students would have a solid, confident low register as a foundation before advancing to the middle (what they often call "high") register. However, students who begin playing as part of an ensemble find themselves above the staff fairly quickly. I define the middle register as being bordered by what many in the Suzuki Flute community call "Bunny Ears D" (because the left-hand pointer and pinky look like ears and the right-hand pinky makes a tail) or D5 and the C-sharp above that (C-sharp6).

With the exception of that D5 and E-flat5, all the fingerings in that register stay the same as their low register counterparts - the register change is purely done with air. This is where the ball toss analogy really comes into play. The higher up above the staff the flutist must play, the further out the student must aim their air while also increasing the amount and speed of that air. I use a line of small animal toys to help students visualize how far out their air has to go for each successive note.

Wrong Register (Too High / Too Low)

Diagnosing what a student is doing wrong to get the incorrect register is pretty simple, as is the fix for the issue. The hard part is coming up with the right combination of words to help them understand what they need to do to change it. What may be obvious to us is not obvious to them, or it wouldn't be a problem. When the wrong register is coming out, the combination of air speed/amount/direction is out of balance and needs to be recalibrated to get the intended result.

Too high (middle register): Air that is too strong/too much and aimed too high will result in a note that is too high, potentially somewhere in the harmonic series above the intended note. E5, F5, F-sharp5, and (somewhat less) G5 are particularly fussy about air and prone to producing the fifth above if approached too strongly. I tell students the flute is saying "too much!" and to back off a little. Sometimes this issue is paired with students puffing their cheeks out and is helped by having them firm up their cheeks/embouchure (rice spitting works really well for this).

Not low enough (low register): Somewhat different than the above issue, which is a student trying for a middle register note and overdoing it, sometimes students try to play a low note (usually F4 and below) and the middle register version comes out. The first place I check is position - if their head is too low, or the flute is too rolled in, the air going across the embouchure hole will be too high regardless of what other factors you change. If their position looks balanced and aligned, they may just need to open their embouchure and slow their air down a bit. Some students achieve the low register by barely blowing at all. This is a means to an end, but creates an issue that must be fixed later on. I prefer to encourage a fair amount of air that is slowed down through a larger, wider embouchure opening and aimed low. Some students respond to the analogy of fogging up a mirror or making a candle flicker without blowing it out. I like to use bubbles, especially with groups of students as a non-flute based exercise for controlling air. Big bubbles can only be made with slow, gentle, low note air.

Too low: The opposite problem to the above requires the opposite solution. In general, students who have trouble playing high are not using enough air and not aiming that air out enough. Often, when they start adding more air into the instrument but before they make it into the middle register, their low register will sound fantastic. This is the indication that they're not using enough air across the board. Giving the student something to aim at that is on the floor but away from them often helps. Some (younger) students respond very well to having a toy (preferably with wings) ride their air. If the sound dips, or never gets high at all, the toy falls.

A long-known trick of flute teachers uses a soda straw* to show students how they can get the octave of a note by simply covering a little more of the embouchure hole with their lower lip. I haven't found this particularly useful for translating to kids what they need to know to actually change their face, but it sure is fun to do. Where I actually find it more useful is to show how the shape of the embouchure hole changes the quality of the tone produced.

Too... not right: Another common issue is a student getting stuck between registers, which produces a growly note that's neither low nor high. This occurs when the student's air isn't low enough to keep the note low but hasn't quite been aimed out enough to make the note high. This can be a useful exercise to do on purpose - to find the line between low and high and ride in the in-between. Sometimes students have to be given permission to sound "bad." Much of the fun of learning a new instrument is the trial and error necessary to find how your own body works with the instrument. I try to emphasize that we are scientists and this is all an experiment. When something doesn't work quite right we gain data that informs our future choices when we play.

*(as written about by Richard Hahn in his article "The Flute Embouchure and the Soda Straw" for the Instrumentalist Hahn, Richard R. "The Flute Embouchure and the Soda Straw." In Woodwind Anthology, vol. 1. Northfield, IL: The Instrumentalist Company, 1999. 191.)

Third Register

After two full octaves of fairly linear fingers (with the exception being C to D) the third octave hits students with the most contrary motion they've ever had to contend with. The more someone has to think about their fingers, the less brain power they can devote to thinking about air (at least, that's how it feels). Unfortunately, this register requires students to use the greatest volume and speed of air. If that air isn't directed down into the flute, all you'll hear is the force of the air and not tone.

Conversely, some students try so hard that they inadvertently roll the flute in and make it virtually impossible to get the note out at all. (My mentor, David Gerry, called this "eating the flute.") I find that having students put more space between their back molars and thinking of a small amount of air between their upper front teeth and top lip helps direct the air down while keeping things open enough to get a big, clear tone.

Buzzing Lips

Sometimes students try so hard to play a note, especially in the high register, their lips emit a spitty, airy, "buzz." This happens when their lips are too tight and they are blowing too much air through too small of an aperture hole. In these cases it's important to help the student to loosen up and allow more air to pass through their lips. I have students put the flute down and do some exercises to relax their lips and cheeks. My favorite ("Horse face" and/or "Zerbert") has the students flap their lips together much like horses do (I believe singers vocalize while doing this as a warmup). I also have them think about imagining a pillow of air between their upper lip and their teeth. Sometimes all it takes is a nice big breath to open their throat and create more space in the back of their mouths.

Support

Many teachers ask their students to "support" but rarely define what that means. This can lead to students tensing their core muscles in a way that actually hinders their breathing and tone production. I tell my students that while we cannot control our diaphragm, we can control the muscles of our abdomen around our diaphragms, thus controlling the speed and consistency of the air we release. Students who cannot activate their core muscles will have a difficult time getting the air speed and consistency necessary to get and stay in the middle register.

Some of my favorite exercises for engaging a student's core is to have them "tsk" rhythms, have them play sitting on an exercise ball, have them play while doing wall squats, and lastly (great for band sections) have them (while sitting) lift their feet off the ground while playing without allowing their backs to touch the backrest.

Dynamics

The need for playing with dynamics comes both too soon and not soon enough. I try to avoid talking about them altogether until the student has a strong, clear, and consistent tone. Many detail oriented students will see the piano marking and immediately stop blowing and force what air they do use between lips that look like they've been sucking on a lemon. This leads to a thin and flat tone that doesn't go anywhere. It also makes it hard to stay in the middle register (which is often where they're supposed to be.) Many of those same students see a forte and overblow, spreading the sound and going stratospherically sharp (if they even stay in the same register.)

Dynamics

Piano: The general rule for dynamics on the flute is that when you put less air into the instrument, you'll get less sound, and vice versa. However, less air does not have to mean slower air or even that the amount of air should change. My teacher from my Master's Degree, Mary Stolper, used to tell us "p means project." In other words, if you raise the air stream to cut across the blowing edge of the embouchure hole higher you'll keep your pitch and tone (and register) while simultaneously sending out a sound that reads as soft even in the back of the auditorium. Therefore, to diminuendo, a flutist has to gradually raise the airstream until there isn't enough air going into the instrument to produce tone at all.

Some students find success by articulating soft notes with a "puh" attack, where they only use enough air and air pressure to part the lips naturally in a "puh" shape rather than using their tongue.

Forte: The lower you can send the air, the more air that gets into the instrument, the louder you'll be (and it will counteract the tendency to be sharp.) To do this and stay in the low register you have to slow the air down (make your embouchure more open) so that you can use a large volume of air without hitting an upper partial.

Vibrato

Vibrato occurs when the player modulates their pitch and dynamic to create waves in their tone. Some students develop a natural vibrato either through listening to great flute playing or luck. Most will play with a straight tone indefinitely or (worse) develop a throaty "nanny goat" vibrato. For ensemble playing, in theory, the principal player sets the style and type of vibrato and everyone either fits into that or doesn't use vibrato at all. Working on vibrato can be really nuanced and probably best left to a private flute teacher, however, sometimes a player's vibrato will make them "stick out" in a section and needs to be addressed. How well your players can control their vibrato can determine how cohesive your section sounds.

While ultimately vibrato appears to come from the throat, I've found it best to encourage students to think of it as coming from their core. This enables them to get a wide modulation in pitch and dynamic while they're slow, making it more likely to continue as they speed up. At the start, I talk a lot about "near" and "far" air, even using my hand as a target to follow with their air. Because  the flute rests against the player's skull, it can be hard for someone to get a sense of how they actually sound in the room. In this case, how wide their modulation or vibrato really is. This is where the spectrometer function on many digital tuner apps comes in really handy. Students, many of whom are visual learners, can see the amplitude and evenness of their sound waves.

The most tried and true way to practice and develop a consistent vibrato continues to be to pulse along with a metronome and then carry that into scales or slow pieces with a measured, or metered, vibrato.

It's difficult to talk to students about dynamics without talking about vibrato and vice versa. This is simply because someone can be playing truly softly and the second they add that wide, church soprano vibrato on top of it, the volume will increase for listeners. Conversely, a student could be blowing all the air in the room into the instrument and without a nice, fat, fast vibrato it just won't come across as loud. Ideally, a player will  develop the control to choose whether to have fast or slow, wide or narrow vibrato. A fast and narrow vibrato will read as soft, a wide and fast vibrato as loud, but there's plenty of room for nuance in between.

Braces

Almost without fail, when a student has something big coming up or is just sounding really terrific, they show up with braces. Many students adjust to braces without any issue at all. Some even sound better. But they can throw some people for a loop. My mentor, David Gerry, taught me his trick for helping with braces: he used masking tape to build up 3-4 layers on the lip plate where the chin goes. There's something about it that helps students adjust to having all the extra room in their mouth taken up by brackets and wires. By the time the tape gets weird and gross the student has figured it out and generally doesn't need it anymore (the lip plate can be cleaned with alcohol). I've  also very successfully used mailing labels for this trick. The key is to make sure to apply whatever you're using to a clean lip plate and to take your time to make sure the tape is smooth and trimmed on the sides nicely.

I tell my students that articulation is like annunciation in English. People can understand you if you say "twenny" but "twenty" will be more clear. Articulation provides a clean start to a note and ultimately allows a player to play more notes faster. Advanced players can change how they articulate and where they place their tongue depending on expressive effect. Players have the choice to tongue between (rice spitting) or behind their teeth but from there where does the tongue go? When and how does someone double tongue and how can the fingers and tongue coordinate?

Between vs. Behind The Teeth

As mentioned in the Embouchure Formation section, I start all my beginners spitting rice. This is known as the "French" or "Between the teeth" style of articulation. (French because of its similarity to the way French people say "tu", between their teeth.) For beginners, teaching this way ensures that they begin notes with their tongue and also promotes a very natural embouchure formation. Many players find the sound of this articulation to be "softer" or "gentler" as it releases the air. As beginners become more experienced their tongue moves from between their lips as when they spit rice to inside their mouth, between their teeth. I've found that sometimes students who use this method of articulation get a little "fuzz" at the start of the note - this usually means their tongue is rolling a little or making a kind of tunnel where the center of the tongue is lower in the mouth than the edges.

The other primary means of articulating a note is behind the teeth, where the upper teeth and roof of the mouth meet. This mimics the English way of saying "tooh." This method offers a really crisp, clear start to notes and allows for great accents. Students who articulate this way sometimes tongue either too far down on their front teeth or too far up onto the roof of their mouth, leading to a dull "thuddy" attack.

Tongue Placement

Most of us don't pay much attention to our tongues until they get in the way and this is true for flutists as well. If the student is getting a strong, clear, uninterrupted sound, their tongue is probably doing just fine. If I think a student may need to adjust where their tongue lives in their mouth I first ask them to try to describe what they feel. Regardless of how someone starts the note (behind or between the teeth), their tongue needs to get out of the way to allow for a column of air to flow for the duration of the note. For most people, this will mean keeping their tongue low towards the bottom of their mouth.

Fuzzy Attacks

Sometimes you'll hear a fuzzy start to a note and you'll realize the student isn't using their tongue at all! When flutists do this intentionally we call it Breath Attacks and it can be a really excellent exercise for coordinating tongue and fingers as well making sure the air is energized and moving at the start of the note. When it's not intentional, even when it's really excellently done, it will end  up being rate-limiting. Tonguing a continuous airstream will always be faster than starting and stopping the air and never really sound crisp or clean.

When the air isn't ready to be released by the tongue, it can create a fuzzy start to the note much like it sounds when a student does not use their tongue at all. This can manifest as a delay between when you hear the air coming out and when the tone actually starts. Ironically, breath attacks are an excellent way to work on this issue but sometimes all it takes is making the player aware that their air is not starting when they tongue the note.

Note Endings

Ending a note on the flute is really quite simple: stop blowing. Sometimes students decide they need to do more work than that and they will add their tongue to the end of the notes (literally "toot"). Not only does this create a hard end to the note, which may or may not be musically appropriate, but it will ultimately be rate-limiting (as the tongue has to do twice as much work for every single note).

Sometimes we want a note ending that is softer or more diffuse than we get from simply stopping our air. This effectively is a fast diminuendo, in which the air has to be raised up from the embouchure hole, essentially stopping the note not by stopping the air but by the blowing edge no longer bisecting the air.

Coordination Of Tongue and Fingers

I'm not sure exactly why a player's tongue and fingers get off-sync from one another, but I do know that it's really common, even for professionals. Fortunately, it's easy to work on, if not exactly intuitive. I joke that the brain tells the tongue to articulate even sixteenth notes (or whatever) and the tongue starts off on that path relentlessly, whereas the fingers have to negotiate contrary motion and process the signals from the eyes to the brain. This causes the tongue and fingers to be out of phase with one another. When this happens, the very best strategy is to actually add slurs. Different slur patterns such as

can broker a truce between the tongue and the fingers and get them working together again. It may take practicing like this more than once for a particular passage, but over time consistency will develop.

Double Tonguing

Double tonguing is the process by which the player utilizes both the initial attack of the tongue and the turn-around motion by employing a second syllable produced by the middle of the tongue such as: kah; keh; ki; ku; gu; gah; etc. For every group of four sixteenth notes, the first and third will have a primary attack (T) and the second and fourth a secondary attack (K).

This is one of my favorite advanced skills to teach and work on with students. My own double tonguing ability is hard-won. I like to tell the story of a Flute Methods student (trumpet player) who asked about double tonguing on the flute. When I demonstrated he said, "Wow, double tonguing on the flute is so easy!" to which I responded, "It took a lot of HARD work to make it sound this easy." That's a long way of saying, if you're considering programming a piece that requires a lot of fast articulation, give your flutists plenty of advance notice. Bonus if your flute section has a high rate of private lesson attendance.

My cutoff line for double tonguing sixteenth notes is around quarter note = 120. Below that I generally single tongue, above I pretty much have to double tongue. That threshold will likely be lower for students, depending on their experience. Many students can single tongue so proficiently that they see little value in double tonguing at first because speed only comes with time and practice. There are four primary areas of concern when troubleshooting double tonguing: 1. the syllables themselves; 2. coordination; 3. stamina; 4. air.

Syllables: Second syllable choice, I feel, is rather personal. I think a lot has to do with a student's home language and what they can do consistently and also what syllable they use to articulate with in the first place. Whatever the second syllable is, whether it starts with a "k" or a "g", the important thing is that the throat never gets involved. Generally when we say the syllables to a student, we vocalize them.  When we vocalize them, that syllable gets placed very far back in the mouth, signaling to the student that our second syllable should be located in back when we take our voices away. This is unnecessary and inefficient. We can interrupt the air and achieve the sound of an articulated note mere millimeters from the initial attack. The more forward we can bring that syllable, the more efficient and faster we can be.

Coordination: By the time students learn to double tongue they will have single tongued probably thousands of notes. That second syllable will naturally be weaker, and potentially uneven. One strategy for counteracting the unevenness is to have the student reverse the double tonguing (K-T-K-T). Another is to have the student just practice starting the notes with only the second syllable. Unless the flutist has spent hours calling for their cat ("here kitty kitty kitty kitty") it is unlikely that they will have had to accomplish this motion repeatedly with their tongues prior to learning this skill. I like to tell my students to practice "TKTKTKTKTKTKTK" under their breath as they're doing mindless tasks like walking the dog to work on the coordination of the tongue itself.

Stamina: There are few stranger feelings than a fatigued tongue, and new double tonguers will find their tongues getting tired. I have students practice in short bursts with space between note groupings in order to make sure they stay focused on getting the best possible sound and most even attacks on every note. As they gain experience and agility those bursts get longer and longer.

Air: Many students focus all their attention on their tongues. They are convinced that there is something wrong with the way they are tonguing. Much (or dare I say most) of the time the issue is actually their air. Notes that are short need faster air to get the instrument resonating than notes that are long. The more you interrupt that air, the stronger the airstream needs to be to keep the tone strong and clear. I take students to the closest drinking fountain to demonstrate the difference between making multiple notes by starting and stopping the water with the push bar versus holding the bar to produce a steady stream of water (or air) and interrupting it by passing your finger (tongue) back and forth. When we add the flute, while the syllables are still slow, I make sure that the notes are very long and they continue to stay long as we increase the speed. This also helps to counteract uneven double tonguing as well.

Double tonguing after a rest: Occasionally a string of notes that need to be double tongued will start with a rest like this:

Without making any adjustments the first note would have a second syllable (K) attack like this:

However, putting two first syllable (T) attacks in a row usually leads to a cleaner sounding result.

Triple tonguing: The principles of triple tonguing are similar to those of double tonguing. The only question is whether the groups of three always begin with a first syllable (T) attack or alternate between first (T) and second (K) syllable attacks

T K T   T K T   vs.   T K T   K T K

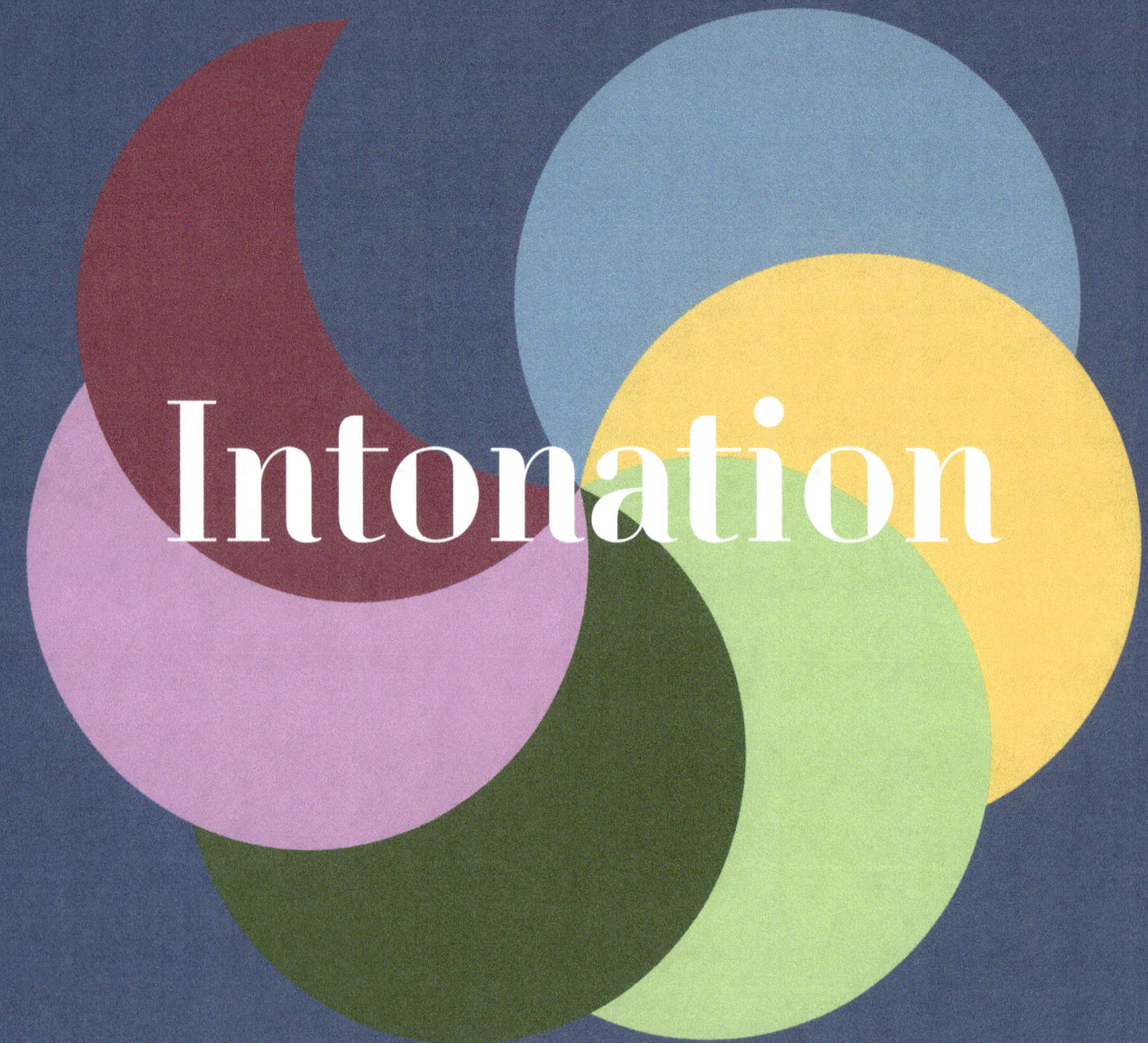

Students with a strong, consistent, supported tone and balanced posture will have fairly centered intonation, assuming their instrument is in working order and of decent quality. Players will notice that how far in or out they place their headjoint will tend to stay within the same range, barring environmental factors (such as a very hot or cold room). Nevertheless, adjustments must be made both before and while playing and more advanced players will want to do more adjusting, depending on register and sometimes even specific notes. Harmonics can be a useful tool for learning how and when to make these adjustments.

Tuning the Instrument

All flutes are made to be put together with the headjoint not pushed all the way in. Let me repeat: headjoints are meant to be pulled out a bit or a lot from the body of the flute. Many students hate not having their headjoint not pushed in as far as it will go, especially if that instrument is plated and the tenon is a different color. Too bad! When tuning the instrument, generally, remember that it is like a string: the longer the instrument is, the lower it will be; the shorter the instrument, the higher. If the flute is sharp (and most of the time it's sharp), pull the headjoint out a bit and try again. If the flute is flat, push the headjoint in and make the tube shorter. When adjusting the headjoint, be mindful of the lip plate alignment with the keys. One of the best, most stable notes to tune to on flute is D5 ("Bunny Ears D") so I usually check the low A (A4), middle A (A5), and then the D.

Intonation Tendencies

Tuning can be an exercise in compromise. While modern flutes have a scale that plays pretty well in tune with itself, the extremes tend to pull away from each other. The low register tends to be flat (and flattest on the lowest notes like C4) and the high register tends to be quite sharp. I try to find the spot where the tuning notes (whether A's or B-flats) aren't too far off in one direction or the other and the D is pretty much spot on. If a student is playing exclusively in one register or another I might weight slightly towards that register's note being more in-tune than the other. Choosing a note to tune to is a snapshot in time and a student who has inconsistent posture or lip placement will have different intonation every time they pick up the instrument.

Typically, soft (piano) playing goes flat and louder (forte) playing goes sharp. As the instrument warms up, it will get sharper. Likewise, it will be sharper in warm environments and flatter in cold ones. General intonation issues tend to be exacerbated by habits students develop as beginners that don't get reexamined as they gain experience and embouchure control. A flat low register or soft notes often come from a student using much less or much slower air than the flute wants because that made it easier to stay low in the beginning. Loud and/or high notes are sometimes blasted out with a very high air stream.

Headjoint Cork

Traditionally the end of the headjoint is sealed with cork. The placement of this cork will change the length of the tube of the headjoint and therefore change the intonation of the entire instrument. If there seems to be a wild (or wider than usual) pitch discrepancy between the low, middle, and high register, that's an indication to check the cork. Flute makers will have a mark on the end of the cleaning rod that when inserted into the headjoint should be centered in the embouchure hole. If it isn't, you can adjust by loosening the crown and either pushing down on the crown to make the cork move towards the open end, or to insert a dowel and push up to move the cork more towards the crown. Be mindful that the cork is not supposed to come out of the crown end of the headjoint (it's ever so slightly smaller than the flute end of the headjoint) so make small movements. Screwing and unscrewing the crown can sometimes shift the cork one way or another so students should be discouraged from fiddling with it when they're bored.

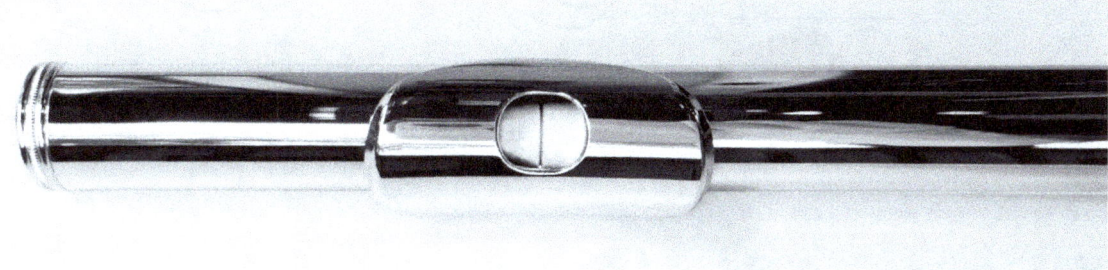

From time to time that cork dries out and will need to be replaced. If you try to tighten the crown of the headjoint and it spins around and around without tightening, that's a clear indication that the cork is no longer sealing. Another way to check is to cover the whole lip plate with your mouth and place your palm over the open end of the headjoint, sucking all the air out. If there's a popping sound when you remove your hand the cork is sealing. If not, it probably isn't and should be replaced.

Some Problematic Notes

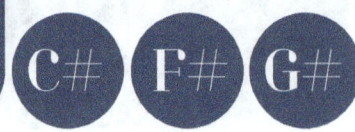

C-sharp: C-sharp has had a long history of being an unpleasant note on the flute. Modern flutes shouldn't have C-sharps that are dramatically out of tune from their neighbors, however, the tone quality is generally weaker or thinner sounding on C-sharp. This can be mitigated by again aiming the air lower into the embouchure hole and creating more space between the back teeth.

F and G-sharp6: There are some fairly standard alternate fingerings for the high register, notably for F-sharp and G-sharp, which can be particularly problematic:

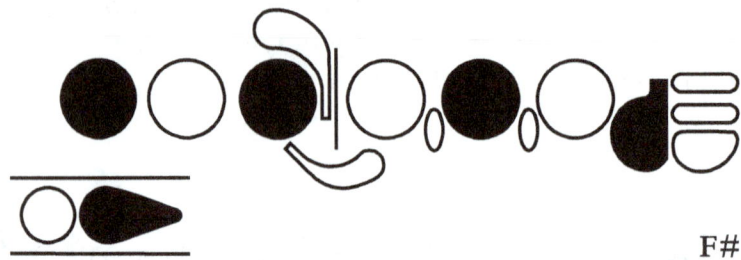

F#

G#

The above fingerings should help lower the pitch and center the tone.

Sometimes, like with D6 or B-flat6, the assumption is that the flute is sharp and it's actually a bit flat. If a student needs a specific accommodation, I love the online fingering chart https://www.wfg.woodwind.org/flute which includes alternate fingerings and best use scenarios (i.e. sharp - good for piano playing, etc)

Harmonics

Harmonics can be a really useful tool for young flutists. Sometimes it's easier for a student to find the necessary air speed and direction for a particular note through the harmonic series. They are also a great way to retrain a student's ear in the third register, as the harmonics tend to have a much lower pitch than the regular fingering. Occasionally a passage is just too fast to be played with the true fingering and harmonics can be considered.

The easiest notes to get the full harmonic series on the flute are the very lowest notes (C4, C-sharp4, and D4), but all low and middle register fingers are capable of producing at least an octave and/or a fifth up. Trevor Wye's *Intonation* book has a nice section on harmonics as does Roderick Seed's *Mastering the Flute with William Bennett*. One of my favorite harmonic exercises comes from my former teacher, Katherine Borst Jones. She would have us play a five note scale and then check the fifth with the harmonic fingering(s). I particularly like to do this with a drone on the tonic.

Ways to Adjust While Playing

Once the instrument seems to be acceptably in tune (the low register isn't horribly flat and the high register isn't horribly sharp) it is up to the player to make adjustments in order to stay in tune with the ensemble (or themselves). For the most part, wherever the pitch needs to go, that's where the air should go. If the note is too flat, the pitch needs to raise and the air needs to raise; if too sharp, the pitch and air both need to lower. Much of this happens with the lips and the spacing between the teeth and experienced players won't even notice they're doing it most of the time. Sometimes bigger change needs to happen and for that moving the whole head up and down is really effective. (Funny side note: the eyebrows seem to have an effect and furrowed brows can help bring the pitch down as raised ones will raise the pitch as well.) Rolling the flute in or out will exact large pitch change as well but should be avoided unless specified for a pitch bend in a piece. Rolling in/out destabilizes a flutist's position and can lead to wrist issues.

Technique

Fingerings on flute are really logical… until they're not. As a general rule, adding fingers will produce lower notes and taking fingers off will give you higher ones. This assumes the fingers are going down and coming up in the correct order and in a coordinated way (minimizing what I call "hitchhiker notes"). Between E4 and C-sharp6 the fingerings stay the same between the low and middle register and every note has one standard fingering (except for B-flat). The system also breaks down at the C5-D5 transition, when it all has to start over again and in the third register. Great technique not only serves the music through note changes, it also allows players to have their best tone on every note.

Finger Order

The modern "Boehm system" flute has been designed to fit our hand and to play twelve chromatic notes using 9 moving fingers (9 fingers that may or may not be located where the hole needs to be to produce that particular note). Pressing one key may make as many as 2 other keys go down simultaneously. This means that while the key work is linear, the fingers may not be, especially for flat and sharp notes. Students who have a piano background, in particular, seem to have some trouble with putting the left hand pointer finger ("Herbert") down before putting their thumb on and vice versa.

B-Flats

B-flat is such an important note for wind and brass players that flutes have three different ways to play it: One & One; thumb B-flat; and lever. Each fingering has advantages and disadvantages and thumb B-flat, in particular, has situations in which it can't be used.

One & One:

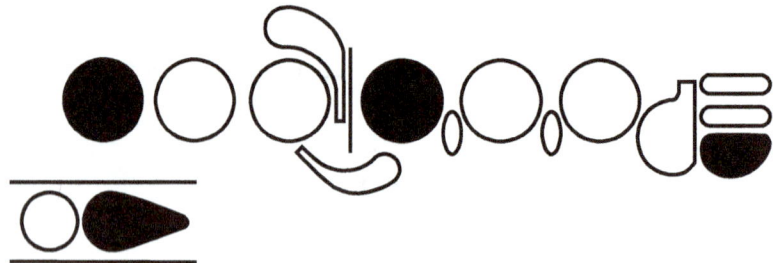

This fingering gets its name from the fact that it is produced using both pointer fingers. This is the first fingering that I teach to my students, primarily because it is the slightly harder fingering to coordinate and I want them to have the most practice using it so they have options when other B-flat fingerings are inappropriate. The drawback to One & One B-flat comes when a player switches to or from a G: if the fingers don't move precisely and F or a B natural will momentarily come out. Sometimes beginners also leave their right pointer down after playing a One & One B-flat, which won't affect an A, but of course turns a G into an F.

Thumb B-flat:

This fingering utilizes a thumb key that causes the key in between the left pointer and middle fingers to depress, thus making a B-flat. This fingering is incredibly useful in passages where all the Bs are flat because, with a few exceptions, it doesn't affect any other note and can be left on for the whole passage. The exceptions are for F-sharp6 and B6. Those are two notes where that key between the left pointer and middle needs to stay open. When it's not open, the pitch and tone quality of those notes suffers. Even fairly experienced students will sometimes forget to take their thumb B-flat off and wonder what's wrong with their flute when they try to play an F-sharp. The other limitation is for passages that do switch between B-flat (or A-sharp) and B-natural. The right hand pointer will always be able to move faster than the thumb will be able to slither and slide between the two keys. Many flutists develop a shorthand in their music to let them know when to use "thb" and when to keep it off "nthb."

Lever:

The lever is an underutilized key towards the headjoint near the right hand pointer key that depresses the key between the left hand pointer and middle fingers. I love using this in chromatic passages and I also introduce A-sharp to my students with this fingering. I've found that it helps minimize the confusion between A-sharp and B-flat, and, because the One & One fingering is usually so ingrained with B-flat, it helps prevent the B-naturals that inevitably come with A-sharp from turning into B-flats themselves. The lever can be pressed while playing a G without affecting the G whatsoever, making it very handy when there are Gs to B-flats and Thumb B-flat isn't an appropriate choice. Lever ceases to be a suitable choice when followed by a note that requires the right pointer to depress the F key, because the finger would need to "hop" between the two.

Contrary Motion

The first experience most students have with contrary motion comes when they have to switch between C5 and D5. I show my students that these fingerings are virtually the opposite of one another: what's up on one is down on the other. The D is a very stable fingering and the C is not, so many students also have an issue with the balance when they transition between those two notes. If E-natural gets added into the mix, the contrary motion becomes isolated to the right hand ring and pinky fingers. Coordinating this motion and developing the balance in this transition is foundational to flute technique and well-worth spending time on.

Left Pointer "Herbert"

Regardless of the notes surrounding D5, students must remember to lift their left hand pointer finger for the D (and return it for any non-C-sharp or E-flat5 note following). When this finger is left down, a D5 could still come out, but it would be a harmonic and therefore unstable and with a different tone quality. This finger is so important my former teacher, Katherine Borst Jones, named it "Herbert" so that we would have a shorthand to know that our left hand pointer was misbehaving!

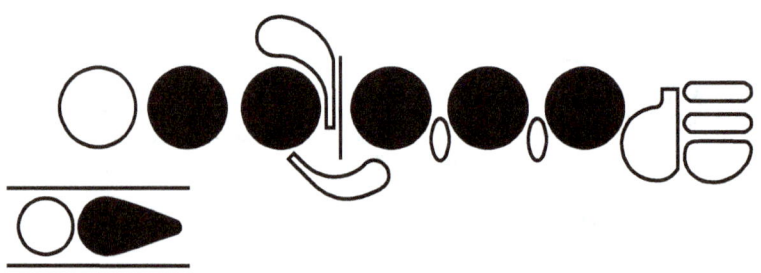

Hitchhiker Notes

Intervals that require a lot of contrary finger movement, especially if that movement involves either of the ring fingers, are prone to getting small, extra notes that come along for the ride. For this reason, I call them hitchhiker notes. I prefer to depersonalize the correction of this issue as much as possible saying, "please ask the right ring finger to work together with the middle finger" or " Herbert seems sleepy today, let's wake him up" rather than something like "you need to fix your left pinky." While by no means a comprehensive list, here are some intervals to be particularly mindful of (and which fingers to watch out for):

- E to F-sharp in the low or middle register (right pointer/middle and ring)
- D to E in the low or middle register (right ring and pinky)
- F to A in the low or middle register (left ring coordinating with right pointer)
- D6 to E6 (left ring and pointer/Herbert)
- E6 to F or F-sharp6 (left middle and ring)
- F6 to A6 (contrary motion in left hand)

Common Fingering Issues

Two of the most common fingering issues (Herbert down on D5 and E-flat5 and and getting extra "hitchhiker notes" between G and B-flat) have been covered in previous sections, but there are plenty more.

Any note around D4&5: Not only does Herbert come up on D5, but so does the right pinky. The right pinky loves its taste of freedom so much it stays up, destabilizing the entire right hand.

E: In anticipation of pinky coming off for the D, students will often prematurely pick up their finger on the E. This will cause the tone to change, especially in the lower register.

F-sharp 4&5: If students have any saxophone experience (and even sometimes if they don't) they discover that they can play a respectable F-sharp with their right hand middle finger (instead of ring). This should be avoided as the ring finger will generally provide a better tone.
Any right hand note preceded by A-flat/G-sharp: Left pinky gets a taste of power (finally) and wants to stay down on every note thereafter, usually resulting in a really hollow tone that isn't the intended pitch.

D6: Once students begin to play above the staff, D6 often becomes a trouble maker. Students often produce D6 as a harmonic of the D5, or forget about Herbert and finger a G.

G-sharp6: Students often take off their thumb but forget to lift Herbert (left hand pointer)

I am not a particularly confident piccolo player and rely on the many great resources dedicated to piccolo playing by expert piccolo players for any serious piccolo questions. That said, ensemble directors need to know some things before asking a player to cover the piccolo part. I personally don't allow students younger than 6th grade to play the piccolo and I prefer if they wait until 7th or 8th if possible. This isn't based in science, it's just my preference for them to have the most developed flute embouchure they can have before adding another instrument, and the piccolo is a second instrument. Rather than "just" a small flute, piccolos have their own unique intonation and tone production quirks. Piccolos come in two keys and a variety of materials such as metal, plastic, resin, and wood.

Piccolo parts look very similar to flute parts as they are written in the same range, but they sound an octave higher. Student piccolos do not have any footjoint keys below D-sharp and cannot play lower than a fingered D4 (sounding D5). The piccolo part is a solo part and will more than likely be heard most or all of the time, so ask a strong player to play. Don't forget to share the wealth, however, as sometimes great players get labeled a piccoloist and never have a shot at juicy flute solos.

Lastly, ear protection is very important for all musicians, and especially piccolo players. Please encourage your students to invest in ear plugs. There are some reasonably priced ones that still allow the player to hear themselves to tune but minimize the frequencies that can damage their hearing. At the minimum, a piccolo player should have an ear plug in their right ear, as it is slightly closer to the loudest sounds.

Types Of Piccolos

In Sousa's heyday it was not unusual for people to have and play piccolos that are pitched in D-flat (rather than C). Sometimes these instruments can be found in the back of instrument closets in well-established programs and don't look any different than a C piccolo to the naked eye. If a piccolo is terribly sharp no matter what the player does, there's a strong possibility that it's a D-flat piccolo!

There are many more material options when purchasing a piccolo than there are for student flutes. The primary considerations have to do with the venue in which the piccolo will mostly be used and budget. Piccolos can be purchased in metal, plastic, composite resin, wood, or any combination.

Metal: solid silver or silver plated piccolos look very much like a flute that's been shrunk down. They are prized for having a responsive high register and are very stable for outdoor playing. In the concert hall their tone can be very piercing, some might even use the word "shrill."

Plastic: Plastic piccolos are a budget compromise that can move from outdoor venues to the concert hall. Their tone doesn't have the depth of wood, but they also don't have the care issues of wood. Plastic piccolos can usually be found with either a matching plastic headjoint or a silver (or silver-plated) headjoint. In this case, the silver headjoint usually provides a brighter sound and a quicker, cleaner attack than the plastic headjoint will.

Composite Resin: Pricer than plastic but less expensive (and less temperamental) than wood, composite resin has emerged as a great option for students, especially ones who play in orchestra. Composite resin has the closest response to wood without actually being wood.

Wood: The gold standard for piccolos in the concert hall is hard wood (often grenadilla wood). A well-played wooden piccolo has a "sweet" sound that blends more easily with a woodwind section than the other materials. As with other wooden instruments, wood piccolos require some special care: they should not be subjected to rapid temperature changes (such as blowing hot air into a cold piccolo or a hot indoor environment to a cold outdoor one) and they should be oiled from time to time.

Tone Production

Students can have a hard time making a consistent sound on the piccolo right away. This is usually because they place the piccolo on their lip in the same spot they put the flute. However, the piccolo is smaller, with a smaller embouchure hole, and many of them don't have lip plates. Placing the piccolo higher on their lower lip usually solves the problem (I try to put the piccolo about center on my lower lip.)

 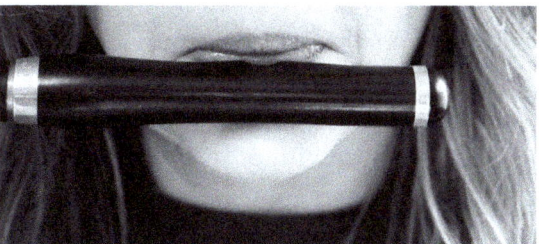

Piccolo also uses air in a slightly different way than the flute. As the piccolo is smaller, it needs slightly less air. However, since the piccolo sounds an octave higher, that air needs to be faster, in general, than a note with the same fingering on the flute. This creates a conflict between what a flutist's eyes tell them what to do with their air and what the instrument needs.

Intonation

Piccolo scales seem to be more variable than on modern flutes, and cheap (or very old piccolos) may not be capable of playing in tune with themselves, much less an ensemble. Players often assume that piccolo will have similar intonation to flute, but just as often a note (or a register) is actually the opposite on piccolo than flute. One example is the high register, which can be flat on piccolo, but everyone assumes that it is sharp and actually exacerbates the issue. The D above the staff (fingered D6) is usually an effective choice for checking intonation.

Many players learn that they have to use different fingerings for notes on piccolo, and there are several resources for finding alternate fingerings on piccolo. Probably the easiest to locate, and the most up to date, is the Alternate Fingering Chart on https://www.wfg.woodwind.org/flute

Buzzing Lips (Piccolo)

I find that piccolo players are even more likely to have trouble with their lips causing a spitty, airy, "buzz." Just like on flute, this happens when their lips are too tight and they are blowing too much air through too small of an aperture hole. In these cases it's important to help the student to loosen up and allow more air to pass through their lips. I have students put the piccolo down and do some exercises to relax their lips and cheeks. My favorite ("Horse face" and/or "Zerbert") has the students flap their lips together much like horses do. (I believe singers vocalize while doing this as a warmup.) I also have them think about imagining a pillow of air between their upper lip and their teeth. Sometimes all it takes is a nice big breath to open their throat and create more space in the back of their mouths. Please watch the flute video on buzzing for examples.

Postscript

Working with students is like trying to untangle a bunch of knotted string. When you pull on one thread, something else tightens and demands attention. A kid who slouches will likely also have inconsistent intonation (and will probably not have a very full tone, either). An educator's hope is to set a kid up in a way that minimizes future issues and future frustration. Our goal is for students to be successful at every step. There is never a better time to fix a concern with a student than now and, with time and attention, there are ways to unravel any issue. The solutions in this book are gleaned from years of experience and years of observing phenomenal teaching, and talking about that teaching with my mentors and colleagues. May *Working with Young Flutists* offer you proven pathways to help your flute students with confidence.

Acknowledgements

From coffee shop conversations with Noah Demland, to editing work by Sarah Bylander Montzka, and trouble shooting with Maria Schwartz and Morgann Davis Parrish, I am fortunate that many talented friends and family helped me make this book a reality. Extra big shout out to Siamak Mostoufi for his discerning eye and valuable input. Many thanks to my designer, Lia Barrett, for her patience with me and her work to make this book both beautiful and usable. Thank you to Michael Summers for the use of the Jupiter® student flute (JFL 700) and his continued support of me as an Altus Artist. Thank you once again to my teachers and mentors, who modeled lifelong learning and to whom I owe my career. Most of all I am forever grateful to my Suzuki Flute colleagues who taught me the power of community and sharing generously.

Altus Artist Meret Bitticks maintains an active schedule as a soloist, chamber musician, and clinician in the U.S. and abroad while on faculty at the Music Institute of Chicago, Lake Forest College, and DePaul University. Ms. Bitticks has joined Trio Chicago and Friends for international concert tours, including the United Arab Emirates and Australia, and has been a regular member of several Chicago-based chamber groups. In 2013 she became the first flutist to receive a Certificate of Achievement for excellence in Suzuki instruction from the Suzuki Association of the Americas and is now one of only a handful of registered Suzuki Flute Teacher Trainers. She studied under Mary Stolper at DePaul University and Katherine Borst Jones at the Ohio State University to earn her Master's and Bachelor's degrees, respectively. She has also traveled to Matsumoto, Japan, to work with Suzuki Flute School founder Toshio Takahashi. A former volunteer at music camps in Haiti, Ms. Bitticks proudly serves on the advisory council for BLUME Haiti, an organization that promotes leadership through music education.

www.ingramcontent.com/pod-product-compliance
Lightning Source LLC
Chambersburg PA
CBHW082214070526
44585CB00020B/2410